Scan the pages with this symbol to collect your portraits. Once you've collected all five portraits, you can display them digitally in your own bedroom!

Scan the pages with this symbol to collect four enchanting element crystals and unlock a secret power that's as special as Elsa's!

THIS IS A WELBECK BOOK
Published in 2019 by Welbeck Children's Limited
An imprint of the Welbeck Publishing Group
20 Mortimer Street, London W1T 3JW

A catalogue record for this book is available
from the British Library.

ISBN: 978 1 78312 497 8
Printed in China
10 9 8 7 6 5 4 3 2

Author: Emily Stead
Designer: Ceri Hurst
Executive Editor: Bryony Davies
Design Manager: Emily Clarke
Production: Nicola Davey

Disney

FROZEN II

An Enchanted Adventure

ELSA
Queen of Arendelle

IN THE NORTH MOUNTAIN,
Elsa learned how to let go and embrace
the icy powers that make her special. With
the help of her sister, Anna, Elsa grew to realise
that together they are stronger and happiness is
not just a dream. Now Elsa faces a new challenge,
a mysterious voice is calling to her and it cannot
be ignored. She must head north across
enchanted lands and into the unknown
if she is to find the truth behind her
magical gift and save Arendelle.

SCAN HERE
TO COLLECT YOUR
Portrait of Elsa!

My destiny is calling

Elsa is the only person that can hear the mysterious voice.

On her journey north, Elsa faces danger at every turn.

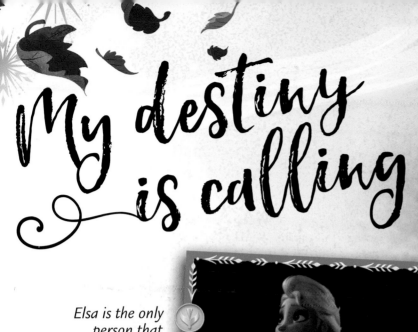

COOL ELSA FACTS

Elsa is surprised to discover that she possesses new magical abilities – she can create special element crystals and ice sculptures that represent memories from the past.

As the elder sister, Elsa was crowned Queen of Arendelle after her parents were lost at sea.

Elsa and Anna each put the other's happiness ahead of their own.

When Elsa is feeling troubled, wearing her mother's scarf brings her comfort.

Unflappable
ANNA

ANNA IS THE MOST CARING
and determined sister a person could
ever wish to have. When she set out on a
dangerous mission to save both her sister,
Elsa, and their kingdom of Arendelle, Anna
proved that only an act of true love can thaw
a frozen heart. Now, as the kingdom faces
danger once again, Anna is desperate to
travel with Elsa on her journey north –
sisters always find a way.

SCAN THIS PAGE
TO COLLECT YOUR
Portrait of Anna!

We do this together

Princess Anna is fearless by nature.

Anna cannot bear to be apart from those she loves.

Brave Anna often rushes into situations without thinking about the dangers.

Anna is friendly and optimistic, always seeing the best in the people she meets.

Anna was thrilled when Elsa declared that the gates to Arendelle Castle should never be closed again.

Kristoff first told Anna he loved her on the princess's nineteenth birthday.

KRISTOFF FACTS

Kristoff was a lonely orphan until trolls Bulda and Cliff raised him as their own.

He used to love nothing more than to roam the wilderness on his high-speed sleigh.

Kristoff once remarked that he thought reindeer were better than people, until Anna's warm heart made him change his mind.

No longer a loner, Kristoff is ready to settle down with Anna, and has even bought an engagement ring to surprise her at the perfect moment.

KRISTOFF

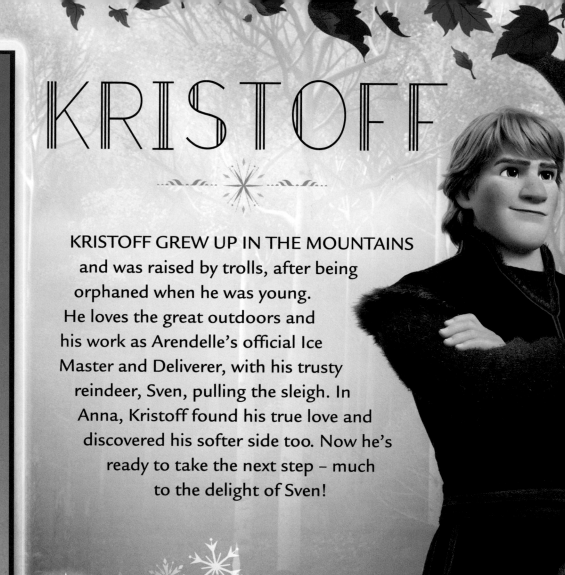

KRISTOFF GREW UP IN THE MOUNTAINS and was raised by trolls, after being orphaned when he was young. He loves the great outdoors and his work as Arendelle's official Ice Master and Deliverer, with his trusty reindeer, Sven, pulling the sleigh. In Anna, Kristoff found his true love and discovered his softer side too. Now he's ready to take the next step – much to the delight of Sven!

SCAN THIS PAGE
TO COLLECT YOUR
Portraits of Kristoff and Sven!

SVEN

SVEN IS KRISTOFF'S OLDEST
and best friend. A reindeer who's
brave and fast, he is an orphan
just like Kristoff. The pair have been
together ever since Kristoff rescued
him as a young calf, and they work
as ice harvesters in Arendelle. Sven is
Kristoff's sleigh-puller, and although
he can't talk, he always manages to
listen to his mountain man friend
and lend support.

SVEN FACTS

Sven's bravery knows no
bounds – the fearless reindeer
has battled snowstorms, freezing
temperatures and crumbling ice
to help those he loves.

Sven is surprisingly fast
and can always be called
upon to race to the rescue
in times of trouble.

Some of Sven's favourite
things include licking
snowflakes and snacking
on carrots!

Sven doesn't always
understand why Kristoff
behaves the way he does, but he
will always stand by his side.

OLAF

OLAF WAS CREATED FROM Elsa's magical powers and is the friendliest snowman in Arendelle! He may not be the most worldly-wise, but his kindness and good humour make him a true friend to Anna and Elsa. He loves being the youngest member of an unusual family alongside Elsa, Anna, Kristoff and Sven. Olaf may be made of snow, but he gives hugs that would melt any heart!

SCAN THIS PAGE
TO COLLECT A
Portrait of Olaf!

Let's Blitz!

COOL OLAF FACTS

Olaf has recently learned to read and loves to share every fact he can remember with his friends. In truth, he's a bit of a snow-it-all.

The little snowman gets befuddled when he loses his carrot nose, but doesn't really notice when Sven tries to crunch it!

Olaf can now survive in any season because Elsa has made him permafrost.

Olaf's friends would describe him as fun and naturally outgoing.

ONCE UPON A TIME, KING AGNARR OF ARENDELLE TOLD ANNA AND ELSA A BEDTIME STORY ...

Long ago, in the far north, lay an enchanted forest, full of magical spirits. Alongside them, a tribe of nomads called the Northuldra lived happily. The Arendellians built the Northuldra a dam as an offering of friendship. When the dam was built, everyone gathered to marvel at its magnificence.

But instead of a celebration, the event sparked a bitter battle between the Arendellians and the Northuldra. This angered the spirits, who turned against both sides. King Runeard of Arendelle fell but his son, the prince, survived. When a haunting cry echoed through the forest, the raging spirits suddenly calmed. Prince Agnarr was returned to Arendelle, where he grew up to become king, while a thick, dark mist swirled up around those who were left behind, stuck in the forest forever.

As King Agnarr finished his tale, his two daughters' eyes were wide. The curious girls were full of questions that remained unanswered.

"Were the Northuldra magical, like me?" Elsa wondered.

But the king could only shrug. He had been young at the time of the battle and had little memory of it.

The girls' mother, Queen Iduna, began to sing a soothing lullaby about a special river called Ahtohallan, said to hold all the answers about the past. Anna, the younger sister, quickly fell asleep.

"Do you think Ahtohallan knows why I have powers?" Elsa asked her mother sleepily.

"If Ahtohallan is out there, I imagine it knows that and much more," the queen replied.

"Someone should really try to find it," Elsa said, as her eyes fell shut.

15

YEARS LATER, THE PRINCESSES HAD GROWN, with Elsa now Queen of Arendelle. Though their parents were gone, Elsa and Anna had found happiness as part of a new family. They loved nothing better than to spend time together with Kristoff, Sven and Olaf.

One autumn evening, the friends were playing a game of charades in the castle library. Kristoff and Olaf were winning – he'd guessed right every time Olaf rearranged: *"Ice cream! Oaken! Elsa!"* he called out.

Meanwhile, Elsa's mind was far away. Anna could tell that something was troubling her sister. *"Are you OK?"* she asked.

"Just tired," Elsa sighed. She quickly excused herself from the game and headed upstairs.

Elsa didn't want Anna to worry. She certainly didn't want to tell her little sister about the voice that had been calling to her, asking her to travel far away. Elsa was happy in Arendelle but a part of her secretly wanted to follow the voice. She tried to ignore it, but the voice would not be silenced.

Moments later, Anna knocked on the door. *"Something's wrong,"* she said.

Elsa tried to put Anna's mind at rest by pretending that she was worried about being a good queen, and said nothing of the mysterious voice.

"You'll always have me," Anna told her sister kindly.

"What would I do without you?" Elsa smiled, climbing into bed.

Anna began to sing their mother's lullaby and soon both sisters drifted off to sleep.

IN THE MIDDLE OF THE NIGHT, ELSA AWOKE TO THE SOUND OF THE VOICE calling to her again. She knew she had to find out who the voice belonged to – what if it were someone magical like her? Without stopping to think, Elsa got out of bed and followed the voice down to the fjord.

As the enchanting voice grew louder, Elsa began to sing back to it. Her hands moved quickly, tracing icy shapes in the air that formed a leaping horse, some children playing and even the forest trees. Never before had she produced such magic!

Spellbound, Elsa used her powers again. This time she blasted out an enormous stream of ice that sent shockwaves across the fjord. *Boom!*

The water in the air suddenly froze, forming hundreds of tiny crystals that hung there magically.

The thunderous boom could be heard for miles around. Back at the castle, Anna awoke. Startled, she raced to the balcony and saw the curious crystals, suspended in the air. Suddenly, a blinding light flashed through the sky from the north, causing the crystals to drop instantly to the ground.

Elsa ran back across the fjord towards the village. The ground began to shake, the fire in all the torches went out, the winds swirled and even the water in the well dried up. Elsa could sense that the spirits of nature were not happy. The villagers came out of their houses, frightened.

SCAN THIS PAGE
TO COLLECT YOUR FIRST
Enchanted Crystal!

ONCE EVERYONE WAS SAFE ON THE CLIFFS ABOVE ARENDELLE, ELSA confessed to Anna about the voice.

"What kind of voice?" Anna gasped. *"What did it say?"*

But the voice hadn't spoken words – it had simply shown her the Enchanted Forest. Elsa knew it was her destiny to travel there.

"Not without us, you don't," Anna said.

Suddenly, the ground began to rumble again, but this time, it wasn't the spirits. What looked like an avalanche of rocks rolled along the path, stopping at the feet of Elsa and her friends. Each rock revealed itself to be a mountain troll.

The leader of the trolls, Grand Pabbie, spoke to Elsa. Both could sense that the spirits of nature were angry.

"*Much about the past is not what it seems,*" he began. "*You must find the truth. Go north, across the enchanted land and into the unknown.*"

Now Elsa had no choice but to find the voice. With Anna and her friends travelling with her, she would not be afraid.

When Elsa's back was turned, Grand Pabbie spoke quietly to Anna. "*Be careful,*" he warned. "*We have always feared that Elsa's powers were too much for this world … now we must hope they are enough.*"

Anna was determined that no harm should come to her sister. "*I won't let anything happen to her,*" she promised Grand Pabbie.

As the sun began to rise, Elsa and her friends began their journey north.

SCAN THIS PAGE
TO COLLECT YOUR SECOND
Enchanted Crystal!

Elsa, Anna, Kristoff, Sven and Olaf travelled further from the kingdom than they ever had before.

Olaf tried to keep everyone's spirits high by shouting out fascinating facts. *"Did you know that water has memory?"* he chirped proudly.

But as the day drew on, the friends became tired of Olaf's chatter. The carriage drove on through the night, until Elsa suddenly called out. *"I hear the voice,"* she said.

Elsa climbed down from the carriage and ran towards a wall of shimmering mist ahead. The others followed. Kristoff put out his hand to touch the mist, but his hand sprang backwards.

Olaf tried next, gathering speed as he approached the sparkling mist. But the snowman bounced straight back, as though the mist were a bouncy pillow.

Elsa reached for Anna's hand. Together, they were stronger. The sisters stepped forwards and the mist parted before them to reveal four towering stones, each with a symbol carved into it – the elements of water, wind, fire and earth.

As the five friends passed the stones, the mist began to change. The sparkling colours faded, and it became thick and grey – they were stuck! Then suddenly, Elsa and her friends found themselves thrown free of the mist, into a clearing.

Olaf cautiously stretched out his arm, it bounced back off the mist, as it had done before.

"It let us in, but it clearly doesn't want to let us out," Kristoff remarked.

"On the bright side, the forest is beautiful," said Elsa.

THE DANGERS OF THE FOREST SOON WENT OUT OF THE FRIENDS' MINDS. OLAF enjoyed wandering in the beautiful surroundings – until he realised that he'd lost his friends. Suddenly, the Wind Spirit appeared, blowing into the forest like a terrifying tornado, and breaking the snowman into pieces.

"*Help!*" called Olaf. Kristoff and Sven raced to help but were swept into the windstorm too. Next, it pulled Anna into its swirling centre.

Elsa desperately tried to use her powers, sending ice and snow in all directions, but the Wind Spirit was too strong. As it swirled tighter and tighter around her, Elsa delivered a powerful icy blast that finally overpowered the spirit.

Snow filled the air and, to everyone's amazement, froze to form a collection of beautiful ice sculptures, each one representing a different moment from the past.

SCAN THIS PAGE
TO COLLECT YOUR THIRD
Enchanted Crystal!

Just then, the trees and bushes began to rustle. Anna quickly armed herself by breaking off an ice sword from one of Elsa's sculptures, and began to make slicing motions through the bushes. Seconds later, an army of soldiers and their reindeer leapt out. They were the soldiers that had been stuck in the forest for all these years – the Northuldra and the Arendellians from King Agnarr's story!

25

TIME, IT APPEARED, HAD NOT HEALED THE RIFT BETWEEN THE TWO PARTIES. The leader of the Northuldra, Yelana, argued with the Arendellian lieutenant, Mattias. Anna, thinking that she recognised Mattias from somewhere, stepped forwards, still holding her sword.

Threatened, both sides rushed towards Anna. Elsa quickly shot out a tremendous blast of ice that knocked the soldiers off their feet.

"That was magic!" Mattias gasped. *"Did you see that?"*

Anna suddenly realised that she knew Mattias from a portrait in the library back in Arendelle. *"You were our father's official guard,"* she addressed him. Mattias's frown broke into a smile.

Yelana was less friendly. She demanded to know what sorcery the girls had used to travel through the mist and awaken the spirits. *"Why would nature reward a person of Arendelle with magic?"* Yelana asked the girls.

Mattias and Yelana began arguing again so loudly that they

SCAN THIS PAGE
TO COLLECT YOUR FOURTH
Enchanted Crystal!

didn't notice a fiery flash running towards them through the trees, setting alight leaves and bushes in its path.

"Fire Spirit!" Yelana cried. Elsa chased after the spirit, spraying snowflakes in every direction to try to stop the fire from spreading. She finally caught up with the animal to discover it was a small, frightened salamander. She held out her hand and the salamander scurried onto her palm. It was soothed by her cool touch. The forest flames flickered out immediately.

Just then, the voice called out once more. Both Elsa and the salamander turned towards it. *"What do we do?"* wondered Elsa.

The salamander looked to the horizon and Elsa instantly understood. *"Keep going north,"* she whispered.

HAT NIGHT, WHILE EVERYONE WAS SITTING BY THE CAMPFIRE, the ground began to shake. From out of nowhere, Earth Giants appeared, causing tremors with each lumbering step. They had come for Elsa. She quickly cast her icy powers into the night sky, sending the Earth Giants in the wrong direction.

Elsa turned to Anna. *"I don't want to put anyone else at risk again. So we're going now, and we're gonna find the voice,"* she explained.

"Where are Kristoff and Sven?" said Anna, worried, but no one knew. With not a second to lose, Elsa and Anna had no choice but to continue their journey north. Olaf skipped closely behind.

They followed the mysterious voice until they reached the wreck of an old Arendellian ship. Anna and Elsa gasped – it was the ship that had once carried their parents! They found a map on board that showed King Agnarr and Queen Iduna had

been heading for the legendary Ahtohallan river – their parents had been seeking answers about Elsa's magic when the storm had broken!

Tears pricked Elsa's eyes. *"This is my fault,"* she cried.

Anna reminded Elsa of her important quest. *"If anyone can save Arendelle and free this forest, it's you,"* she said. *"I believe in you more than anyone or anything."*

Elsa vowed to make it across the Dark Sea and find Ahtohallan ... but she knew she must do it alone.

In a flash, Elsa conjured a boat made of ice under Anna and Olaf and sent them sliding down a path of ice. Anna desperately tried to steer the boat onto dry land, but it was no use ... the ice boat was carried down the rolling river and over a waterfall ...

TIRED AND ALONE, ELSA FINALLY REACHED THE NORTH. SHE STOOD AT THE edge of the Dark Sea, her eyes staring out at the crashing waves. Taking a deep breath, she sprinted into the freezing waters, while blasting out a huge path of ice before her. But the waves were too strong and swept Elsa deep underwater.

Suddenly, a flash of lightning lit up the dark waters – a horse-like creature shimmered close to Elsa before disappearing in a second lightning flash. The Water Spirit! Elsa swam to the surface and scrambled onto a small iceberg. But the creature followed and shattered the ice, tossing Elsa back into the water. The two battled, above and below the freezing waves.

Then Elsa used her magic to create a bridle made of ice. She grabbed the reins and hauled herself onto the Water Spirit's back. It reared up in the water, but Elsa's

SCAN THIS PAGE TO
create magic before your eyes,
JUST LIKE ELSA!

30